Will

PRAISE FOR *STORYSHARES*

"One of the brightest innovators and game-changers in the education industry."
– Forbes

"Your success in applying research-validated practices to promote literacy serves as a valuable model for other organizations seeking to create evidence-based literacy programs."

- Library of Congress

"We need powerful social and educational innovation, and Storyshares is breaking new ground. The organization addresses critical problems facing our students and teachers. I am excited about the strategies it brings to the collective work of making sure every student has an equal chance in life."
– Teach For America

"Around the world, this is one of the up-and-coming trailblazers changing the landscape of literacy and education."
- International Literacy Association

"It's the perfect idea. There's really nothing like this. I mean wow, this will be a wonderful experience for young people." - Andrea Davis Pinkney, Executive Director, Scholastic

"Reading for meaning opens opportunities for a lifetime of learning. Providing emerging readers with engaging texts that are designed to offer both challenges and support for each individual will improve their lives for years to come. Storyshares is a wonderful start."
- David Rose, Co-founder of CAST & UDL

Will

Cynthia Kerns

STORYSHARES

Story Share, Inc.
New York. Boston. Philadelphia

Published in the United States by Story Share, Inc.

Storyshares
Story Share, Inc.
24 N. Bryn Mawr Avenue #340
Bryn Mawr, PA 19010-3304
www.storyshares.org

Inspiring reading with a new kind of book.

Interest Level: Middle School
Grade Level Equivalent: 2.5

9781642612226

Book design by Storyshares

Printed in the United States of America

Storyshares Presents

1

Without opening his eyes, Dylan swung out his arm and hit the snooze button on his alarm clock. "Ten more minutes," he mumbled to no one.

Bam! Bam! Bam! Bam!

Dylan groaned. He pulled the covers over his head. *Just ignore him and he'll go away*, he thought.

Bam! Bam! Bam! Bam!

"Shut up, Jeff!" Dylan yelled from under the covers.

He waited, tense. All was quiet. He smiled. Good. He started to fall asleep.

BAM! BAM! BAM! BAM!

Jeff now stood just to the side of Dylan's bed.

"Shut up!" Dylan said. He tried to grab his younger brother.

Jeff quickly ran away. "Mom! Dylan tried to hit me!"

"Dylan! Time to get up!" his mother called from the kitchen.

The alarm went off again.

"Great," Dylan mumbled.

He felt under his bed and pulled out a pair of jeans. He threw them back down. Wrong pair. His hand reached deeper under the bed until he nearly fell over its side. He crawled halfway under his bed before he found his favorite jeans.

He looked in the mirror as he ran his hands through his short, brown hair to get rid of the matted tufts from sleeping on his side.

"Kelly! Are you almost done in there?" he asked, shaking the dust off his jeans.

"How did you know I was in here?" Kelly yelled from the bathroom.

"You're always in there!"

"Shut up! I'll be out in a minute."

2

"Why can't Kelly use your bathroom?" Dylan asked his mom when he walked into the kitchen.

"Good morning," Mrs. Patterson said cheerfully.

"I'm serious!" he said. He poured cereal in his bowl. "She's always hogging the bathroom."

"There's only the three of you. When I was your age, I had to share the bathroom with four others."

"So?"

"So. If we could share, so can you."

Kelly walked into the kitchen. She moved her head so her dark ponytail swung side to side. Kelly and Dylan had the same brown hair and the same brown eyes as their dad. Jeff had red hair and brown eyes, like Mrs. Patterson.

"It took you that long in the bathroom to put your hair in a ponytail?" Dylan said.

Kelly glared at him. "At least I care about how I look."

"What do you mean?"

"I mean all you wear are sweatshirts. And you're wearing the same jeans you wore yesterday."

"They are not the same jeans!"

"Kids! Enough!" Mrs. Patterson said.

"Can I spend the night at Emma's on Friday?" Kelly asked.

"Will her parents be there?"

"Her mom will."

"I suppose it's all right," Mrs. Patterson rinsed out her coffee cup. "I'll call her mom tonight or tomorrow," she promised as she pulled Jeff's lunch from the refrigerator.

"You're not going to Dad's?" Dylan asked in surprise. "How come?"

Kelly poured milk on her cereal. "I don't want to hang out with Dad on Friday night. And the last time I was with Dad, he criticized everything about me."

"He didn't criticize you about *everything*," Dylan argued.

Kelly shrugged. "He kept asking all kinds of questions about my friends. Said they were probably bad influences. He didn't like the way I styled my hair. I'd rather be with my friends and having fun than be with Dad."

Kelly and their dad fought more than they used to. In a way, Dylan was almost relieved she was going to be with friends.

From the kitchen window, he saw the street corner. Three students stood there: two girls and a boy. Dylan stared as a long, orange bus pulled up to meet them. The two girls climbed in. The boy looked behind him, then climbed in after them. The bus tires squealed as it pulled away from the curb.

Dylan put his bowl in the sink, then grabbed his backpack and skateboard by the door.

"I'll pick you up at 4:00 for your dentist appointment," Mrs. Patterson reminded him.

"Can you pick me up at the park?"

"Only if you promise you'll be watching for me. I don't want to have to hunt you down."

He nodded and pushed out through the door. Five houses lined their cul-de-sac. Dylan's house was the second from the end and looked like all of the others. Single-story brick homes, with the garages attached at the right. Every house had at least one tree in the yard. His big tree stood between his yard and the yard next door.

He slung his backpack over his shoulder, dropped his skateboard on the sidewalk, and kicked off.

3

The morning was perfect. Yellow and red leaves stood out against the gray sky. The leaves that fell on the sidewalk crunched under his skateboard wheels. The wind swooshed in his ears. He turned his baseball cap backwards on his head, so it wouldn't fall off, and rode faster.

School buses passed him. A few heads poked out of windows and yelled "Hi."

He was glad he didn't yet have to take a bus. He would, when he went to high school two years from now.

The high school was on the other side of town. His mom would never let him skateboard that far. But Kelly would have her driver's license by then. Their mom promised that when Kelly got her license, she'd buy a new car and let Kelly have her old one. Maybe Kelly would let him ride with her.

Dylan steered his skateboard to the left. He let his mind go blank as he sped over the sidewalk. The whir of the wheels over the concrete almost hypnotized him. The park appeared on his left.

He veered expertly onto the path that cut through the center. Here, the leaves made a padding for his wheels. They whispered rather than whirred. Trees blocked the noise of traffic. He wished he could keep skating. Blow off school and stay here, where it was cool and quiet and...

A rock buried under the leaves caught in his front wheel. Dylan leapt off his skateboard. He landed on his feet, but his speed kept him going another four or five feet until eventually he hit the pavement.

"Have a nice trip?"

Four eighth-graders hung around the swingset. One of them had his cellphone pointed towards Dylan.

Dylan wiped the dirt off his pants. "Stupid stoners," he muttered.

He picked up his skateboard and walked towards the school. At least no one else saw him. They would most likely forget all about him before first period.

Since it was Wednesday, social studies was Dylan's first-period class. Jenny always sat in front of him in first period. He hoped she wore her pink sweater today. She hadn't worn it yet that week.

4

The rectangular-shaped school stretched half a block in length. Its parking lot ended on the back side of the park. It was just off a four-lane main thoroughfare. A small store stood between the school and the road. Except for the store and school, the rest of the neighborhood was residential. Uniform ranch houses lined the streets.

Fluorescent lighting dimly lit the inside of the school. Dark blue paint covered the walls of the hallways. Gray lockers lined the corridors, interrupted only by classroom doors. Windows belonged to the classrooms. A pattern of black and white checkered the floor.

Occasionally, an open classroom door exposed a shock of sunlight from outside. The usual effect was of artificial light and shadows.

"Today already sucks!" Trevor said. He dropped his backpack on the floor.

"Why?" Dylan shoved the bag away. "Let me get my stuff out first. OK?"

He'd been excited the first day of school when he discovered that Trevor had the locker right above his. They had first met last fall at 6th grade orientation. Dylan hadn't wanted to admit how scared he was, or embarrassed. He'd walked into the gym and seen everyone else sitting with at least one parent. Both of his parents had needed to work, so he had gone alone.

That's when he'd noticed Trevor sitting by himself. His mom hadn't been able to go, either. They'd fast become best friends.

Last year, when their lockers were a row apart, Trevor's messy style had been funny to Dylan. Now, it was annoying.

Trevor shrugged. "I can just tell. I have English first period. I hate Ms. Nichols."

"She's not that bad," Dylan said. He shoved his backpack and skateboard into his locker.

"She's always carrying that stupid clipboard and writing notes whenever she talks to me."

Dylan grinned and slammed his locker shut. "All done."

Trevor opened his locker. Two notebooks and a book fell out. "Crap! Told you it was going to be a lousy day."

Dylan laughed. He bent down to pick up the papers as Trevor tried to pull out his books without dropping anything on his friend's head.

"Hi, Dylan."

Dylan knew from the nasal, whiny voice and the brown loafers who it was.

"Hi, Gary."

Standing beside Gary, Dylan felt tall. Gary was the shortest kid in the 7th grade. He reminded Dylan of a snowman on stilts. Roly-poly on top, but with thin legs. His short, red hair was combed and slicked to one side. His thick, black-framed glasses magnified his blue eyes.

"How come you never take the bus anymore?" Gary asked.

Dylan shrugged. "I told you last week. I like to skateboard."

"Lucky!" Gary hit the top of his notebooks. "I wish my mom would let me have a skateboard."

He fell suddenly into the lockers.

5

"Skateboard?" said a voice behind him. "You can't even stand up straight."

Gary, his face bright red, gave a small smile. "Hi, Josh," he said softly.

To Dylan, Josh Logan seemed to be more than one person. Everyone knew him. Even Kelly and her friends,

8th graders last year, all knew and liked Josh, a mere 6th grader.

Josh never looked like anything bothered him. He had light brown hair that was parted on the side and bangs that swooped just over his eyebrows. His brown eyes were a little too wide apart, making him look like he was always surprised. Wide, thin lips formed a permanent smirk. His clothes were casual and neat. Even when playing sports, he never looked dirty or sweaty. Girls liked him, even older girls. Dylan wasn't sure why.

"He's got appeal," Trevor once said.

"What does that mean?" Dylan asked.

Trevor shrugged. "I don't know. I just heard my sister say that about a guy she likes."

Josh was never alone, either. He always had three or four people following him. Today, his best friend Tony stood next to him. Ben and Tim stood just behind Tony.

After knocking Gary into the lockers, Josh helped him stand up straight. "Look, we're just kidding with you. No hard feelings, okay, buddy?"

Gary blushed. "Yeah, sure. Bye, Dylan."

"Bye, Dylan," Josh imitated Gary's nasal voice.

"You shouldn't be so mean to him, Josh," Dylan said.

He didn't understand why Josh bothered with Gary. He hadn't had a problem with him last year.

"I'm just playing with him," Josh said. "Besides, he's not, like, a friend of yours or anything."

"Does he have any friends?" Tony asked.

"Oh, yeah, right." Josh nodded. "What's up, Trevor?"

Trevor shrugged. "English first period."

"That sucks," Josh said. He smiled at Kathy as she passed him in the hall. "She's gotten bigger just since school started."

"Jesus, Josh," Dylan giggled.

"Hey, it's just nature," Josh imitated Mr. Pence, the science teacher, quoting his health lecture on puberty. The others laughed.

"Good morning, boys!"

All four turned. Ms. Thane, the principal, stood behind them, her arms folded across her chest. Her gray pants, white shirt, and gray hair matched the door of the school.

"Good morning, Ms. Thane!" Josh said politely. "How are you today?"

"I'm fine, thank you, Josh." She smiled. "Have you four noticed the halls are almost empty?"

Dylan looked at the clock. 8:13. Two more minutes and they'd be late.

"Yeah. Sorry about that," Josh apologized. "We were helping Trevor get his books out of his locker. He couldn't find the right notebooks."

Ms. Thane sighed. "Trevor, perhaps this afternoon you should clean out your locker before you leave."

"Yeah, Trevor, your locker really is a mess!" Josh agreed.

Ms. Thane smiled again. "Get to class, boys."

"Have a nice day, Ms. Thane!" Josh called after her.

Tony punched him in the arm.

"What?" Josh asked. "She's nice." He smiled sideways at Dylan as they walked into the classroom.

Dylan moved to the back of the room.

Jenny was already in her seat. Her back was to him while she talked with Winnie, sitting next to her. Her brown hair was pulled back in a ponytail. He liked it when she wore it down.

I'll wait for her to say hi first, he thought.

"Hi, Jenny," he blurted out.

Jenny turned to him and smiled. "Hi, Dylan."

She wasn't wearing the pink sweater, but the blue shirt. It matched her eyes.

6

"How was English?" Dylan asked.

He sat at the end of a long table with Trevor, Adam, and Mike. The table was the second to last in the room, furthest from the doors. Ms. Thane and two office aides wandered the room, watching the students.

It always took Dylan a couple of minutes to get used to the stale air of the cafeteria. It smelled of a jumble of grease, milk, plastic, and trash.

"OK," Trevor mumbled, his mouth full of chicken. "Any homework in social studies?"

"Just a reflection on what we read in class." Dylan looked around the cafeteria. As usual, Jenny sat three tables away with her friends.

"What's so funny over there?" Adam looked toward the other end of the table, where Josh sat surrounded by Tony, Kathy, Eva, Ben, and Joe.

Josh saw Dylan and waved. "Hi, Dylan!" he called in a nasal voice. "You're so lucky you get to ride a skateboard! I want a skateboard, too!"

Dylan's face burned. He quickly looked away from Josh.

Adam snorted his milk. "That's awesome!"

"I wish my mom would let me! It's not fair!" Josh slapped the table with his hand. Everyone laughed.

At the next table, right behind Josh, Gary stood up.

"Hi, Gary," Ben called.

Josh swung around. "Are you done eating?" he asked Gary. "Sit over here, buddy. Move over, Tony!"

Gary shook his head. "That's OK. I gotta go."

Dylan dropped the rest of his hamburger onto his tray. His stomach churned. He looked away from Gary as he walked by. He felt embarrassed for him.

Josh watched him walk away. "That is one troubled kid," he announced. The others agreed.

* * *

"Carrie said Tara didn't say that."

"That's not what Ben said. He said that Laura heard her say it."

"When?"

"Monday in Spanish."

"Laura was absent Monday!"

Dylan huddled with the others at his table. They all held their books up right in front of their faces. Ms. Nichols spoke with Gary at a table on the other side of the room.

John whispered, "All I know is that Ben said Laura heard her say it."

"How could Laura hear her when she was absent?" Colin repeated his question slowly.

They all turned and looked at Tara at the next table. Tara paused, pulling her hair back in a ponytail.

"What?" she hissed.

"'What' yourself?" Colin asked.

"Tables five and six!" They all jumped. "If you keep talking," Ms. Nichols warned, I'll have to keep you after class!" She wrote something on her clipboard.

Dylan turned back to his book. He saw Josh looking at him from another table. Josh made a face at Ms. Nichols' back. Dylan snickered. Josh leaned in closer to the others at his table. He whispered something and pointed. Dylan looked.

Stacy sat in her usual corner table. She absently twirled the ends of her hair in her fingers as she stared at the open book in front of her. She'd been reading the same book for two weeks. Her white socks were pulled up over the ankles of her green sweatpants. Her blue-striped shirt slipped off her shoulder, exposing her white bra strap.

Josh sneezed. "Fatty!" flew out with his sneeze. Those sitting near him laughed.

Colin turned and looked at him through his green bangs. "Dude, that's not right."

Ms. Nichols stood up. "Right! Thanks to Colin and the others at tables five and six, everyone gets to stay back this afternoon."

Colin shrugged as Ms. Nichols made another note on her clipboard. "That's not fair!"

"Hey, guys! Don't argue and just be quiet so we can all leave," Josh announced.

"Thank you, Josh," Ms. Nichols said. "The rest of you should follow his advice."

Josh winked at Dylan.

7

"What time is your mom coming?"

"4:00. Hurry up!"

Dylan stood behind Trevor, trying to avoid being pushed by all the other students rushing to their lockers. Because Ms. Nichols made them stay after, Trevor got to the lockers first.

"I'm hurrying!" Trevor rummaged in his locker. "Nope. Nope. Not that one. Yes! There it is!" He yanked out a notebook.

"Ow!" Mattie glared up at him as she rubbed her head.

"Sorry." He picked up his reading book and shoved it in his backpack. "All done! Meet me at the park."

"Wait for me!" Dylan called. Too late. Trevor was already heading for the exit.

That was real nice of him.

Dylan looked up. His face reddened.

"Hi, Jenny." *Thank God Trevor left!* He quickly threw his books in his backpack and grabbed his skateboard. "Are you on your way home?" he asked as he stood up.

She shook her head no. "I'm going to study group, then volleyball."

"Oh." He couldn't think of anything else to say.

"Why don't you come to study group?" she asked.

Dylan shrugged. "It's boring."

He used to go at the beginning of 6th grade. But he felt uncomfortable. Everyone else was able to do their work on their own. He kept having to ask for help from the staff.

"Oh. Well, I like it. I get my homework done early."

"Oh," he said again. He looked around the hall. *How did it get so empty so quickly?* "I'm going to the park right now." His voice sounded like the dog from *Up*.

"To do what?"

Dylan shrugged. "I don't know. Hang out. My mom's picking me up at 4:00."

"Oh."

He looked at the book in her hand. "What are you reading?"

She showed him. *The Book Thief.*

"Is it any good?" he asked.

"It's really good. What about you?"

He nodded. "Goosebumps."

"Oh, yeah! I read those in 5th grade." Her eyes widened. Her face turned red. "I mean, I like those books, too."

Dylan swallowed. He felt his cheeks grow red, too. He shifted the weight of his skateboard. "Well, I gotta go. See you tomorrow."

"Bye! See you tomorrow!" she called after him.

8

"Why are we sitting here?" Colin asked.

"Because I promised my mom I'd look out for her," Dylan explained again.

"Why?" Colin shrugged. "It's just kind of boring sitting right by a parking lot."

Trevor spat in the dirt. "It's just as boring sitting anywhere else." He spat again. "How long do you want to grow your hair?"

Colin's hand went up to his hair. It almost reached his shoulders. "Not much longer. I want the green to grow out more before I put in purple."

Trevor's hand went up to his own short, curly, blond hair. "How would I look with purple hair?"

"Like a sheep with purple hair," Colin said.

Dylan laughed again.

Trevor looked at Colin. Then, with a yell, he jumped on top of him. Colin easily pinned Trevor on his stomach.

"Do you give up yet?" Trevor muttered, his face plastered in the ground.

Colin rolled off of him, laughing with Dylan.

"You guys look gay!"

Dylan looked up. Josh was walking towards them.

"Jesus, Josh!" Colin exclaimed.

"What? I didn't say it was bad!" Josh playfully swiped Colin's hair.

"That was pretty crappy, you getting us in trouble today," Colin said.

Josh held up his hands innocently. "Hey, all I did was sneeze. Ms. Nichols heard your big mouth."

"Whatever!" Colin picked up his jacket. "Your mom's here, Dylan."

He walked away, heading towards the city bus stop.

Dylan picked up his bag. "Talk to you later, Trevor."

He walked to the car.

"I didn't know you were still friends with Josh," Mrs. Patterson said as they drove away.

Dylan stared out the window. "What?" he finally asked. "What's wrong with Josh?"

Mrs. Patterson lifted her hands innocently from the steering wheel. "I didn't say there was anything wrong with Josh."

Dylan knew what the look on her face meant. "You don't like Josh."

"I never said that!"

"You don't have to." He sat quietly for a moment. "Why don't you like him?" he asked after a long pause. "He's one of the most popular kids in school. Even Kelly and her friends liked him when they were 8th graders last year."

"I know. I remember you saying he was popular last year." Mrs. Patterson thought for a moment. "It's not that I don't like him. I don't trust him."

Dylan was stunned. "He wouldn't steal anything."

"I don't mean that," she said. "He just doesn't seem as real as Trevor or Colin. By the way, what color is Colin's hair? I couldn't tell."

"Green."

Mrs. Patterson laughed.

"I don't get it," Dylan said. "You like Colin, a guy with green hair, and Trevor, but you don't like Josh."

"Again, I didn't say I didn't like him," Mrs. Patterson repeated slowly. The same way she explained something to Jeff. "He's very polite. I just sometimes think he's not always who he pretends to be."

Dylan didn't say anything. It bugged him when his mom was right.

9

"David Lewis posted a picture of you on Facebook."

Kelly sat across the table from Dylan. Her smile grew bigger.

"Doing what?" Mrs. Patterson asked. She passed Kelly her plate.

"Falling off his skateboard!" Kelly almost screamed.

"I want to see!" Jeff demanded.

"Were you skateboarding on the street?" Mrs. Patterson asked.

"No. I fell in the park," Dylan said.

It was true. He fell in the park. Not when he was skateboarding on the street.

"I want to see!" Jeff yelled again.

"No," Mrs. Patterson said.

Dylan silently thanked her.

"Not until after dinner," she added.

"Mom!" Dylan yelled.

Mrs. Patterson shrugged. "If you're old enough to ride your skateboard all over, you're old enough to accept the consequences."

It wasn't a picture, but a video. Dylan didn't know until he saw it in the recording that he'd screamed "Crap!" right before he hit the ground.

"How did you not know this was online?" Kelly asked.

"If I had a cell phone I'd know," Dylan muttered, loud enough for his mom to hear.

"You know the rules. No cell phone until 16."

"But everyone has one!" Kelly wailed. "It's not fair we have to wait."

"Wipe off the dishes before you put them in the dishwasher, Kelly," Mrs. Patterson said. "What you guys don't understand is how much freedom we had without a cell phone. When we left the house, we were gone. Our parents couldn't get hold of us. We could be gone for hours without them knowing where we were. That was freedom. Your dad and I want you to have that same experience."

"No, you and dad are just cheap and don't want to pay for it," Kelly muttered.

"That's enough, Kelly!" Mrs. Patterson snapped.

"What if someone tries to kidnap me and I can't call you?" Kelly demanded.

"Let's hope that happens before you turn 16," Dylan said.

Kelly glared at him.

"Maybe someone would put it on Facebook," Jeff offered.

Mrs. Patterson smiled. "That's true. We can always keep tabs on you through Facebook. Thanks to me," she added, looking pointedly at Kelly.

"That's because Facebook is free," Kelly said.

Mrs. Patterson stopped smiling. Jeff and Dylan looked at each other.

Uh-oh, Dylan thought.

Mrs. Patterson inhaled and exhaled slowly. "Finish the dishes and do your homework," she said.

She left the kitchen without looking at any of them. A moment later, they heard her door slam shut.

"That was a mean thing to say," Dylan said.

Kelly opened her mouth just as the phone rang.

"I'll get it!" Jeff yelled. He raced to the phone. "Hello? Yeah? OK. Kelly! Telephone!" Jeff held up the phone.

Kelly glared at Dylan as she took the phone. "Hello? Hi! I know! He looks like a complete idiot!"

Dylan slammed his bedroom door shut. No point in checking his email. He knew what the messages would say.

10

"Dude! That was hilarious!"

"Thanks, Trevor," Dylan muttered. He shoved his books in his locker.

"I mean, you really wiped out!" Colin said.

"It wasn't that bad," Dylan said. He stuck his head further into his locker.

"The way you fell off, you looked like a goose running. Your neck all stretched out, arms flapping like wings!" John demonstrated. The others laughed.

Maybe I'll tell the nurse I'm sick and have to go home, Dylan thought. He pulled out the last of his books, stuffed his backpack in his locker, and slammed it shut.

"Hi, Dylan!" Gary stood at his locker. "I saw you on Facebook. That looked like it hurt."

"You are on Facebook?"

Tony and Josh walked up behind Gary. Gary stopped smiling.

"Of course Gary's on Facebook," Josh answered Tony. "Haven't you received any of his famous friend requests? I think you've sent one to everyone in school, haven't you, Gary?"

Gary turned to leave, but Josh put his arm around his shoulder. "What I want to know is, who actually agreed to be your friend? Who would possibly friend you?"

Gary glanced around for help. His eyes met Dylan's. Dylan looked away. Gary's head dropped.

Josh squeezed Gary's shoulders. "Hey, just kidding, buddy! No need to get upset."

Dylan waited at his locker until the others left for class. "I'll talk to you later, Gary. OK?"

Gary nodded once. Dylan moved away. Halfway down the hall, he stopped and turned around. Gary still stood at the lockers, staring at his brown shoes.

11

The last class of the day was math. Dylan stared at the clock on the wall.

"Mr. Chapin!" Gary called. "You forgot to write on the homework board to answer the two additional problems on the website."

"Jesus, Gary!" Tony moaned.

"What the hell are you doing?" Josh yelled.

"I would have remembered," Mr. Chapin said calmly. "Thank you for the reminder, Gary." Mr. Chapin looked at the clock. "3:00. Class dismissed."

The only good thing about having Mr. Chapin's math class for the last period of the day was that his clock was three minutes fast. Mr. Chapin never waited for the bell. He dismissed class when his clock ticked 3:00.

Dylan tried to catch Jenny's attention as he walked out of class. She was talking with Winnie again. He hoped to speak to her in the hall before the other classes let out. He followed her and Winnie toward the lockers.

"Josh Conway!"

Dylan jumped. Winnie and Jenny spun around. Dylan suddenly turned to the drinking fountain.

Josh stopped talking with Tony. "Yes, Ms. Thane?"

"Can you come with me, please?" Ms. Thane led Josh to her office.

Dylan watched Josh follow her. By the time he turned back around, the bell had rung.

Students swarmed out of the classrooms. They reminded Dylan of ants rushing out of a hill that had been kicked. He hurried to his locker. Jenny was nowhere in sight.

"Ouch! Dammit, Trevor!"

"Sorry!"

The halls were empty when Dylan slammed his locker shut. He saw that Josh was still in Ms. Thane's office and decided to go out the exit just past there.

As he walked by, he heard Josh say, "Honestly, Ms. Thane. I would never do anything to Gary! He's a good kid. I feel kind of sorry for him."

12

"I still can't believe you can't go to the football game tomorrow night!" Trevor moaned.

They stood outside the store, waiting for it to empty. It seemed like half the school was inside.

"It's not my fault. Friday nights I have to be with my dad."

"I know. It's just that tomorrow night is going to be great!" Trevor pumped his fist for emphasis.

Dylan didn't think so. He was glad he had an excuse not to go. No one who went to a game really watched the game. Going to a high school football game meant walking under the bleachers and through the concession stand all night, talking to people he didn't really know or like. Dylan thought it was boring.

"I'll come over Saturday, OK?" he told Trevor.

Trevor hit Dylan in the arm. "Look who's coming."

Jenny and Winnie came towards them.

"What are you doing here?" Dylan blurted out.

Jenny stopped smiling. "Thanks a lot."

"I didn't mean that," Dylan stammered. "I just meant I've never seen you here before."

Jenny shrugged. "I didn't feel like going to study group. Too hungry."

"Are you going to the game Friday?" Dylan asked, just to say something.

"What game?"

Dylan stared. *Was she kidding?* Then he remembered she just moved to the area over the summer. "Kennedy against St. Luke's. It's kind of a big rivalry here."

"Oh." She shrugged. "I'm not really that into sports. Are you going?"

He shook his head. "I have to go to my dad's. During the school year, we see him every Friday night."

"Since we moved I only see my dad once a month, and during vacations. Are you mad you can't go to the game?"

Dylan looked at Trevor. He was talking to Winnie. Dropping his voice to make sure Trevor couldn't hear, he said, "I'm not that into it, either."

"Are you going to the store?" she asked.

"Yeah. Do you want me to get you something?" he asked hopefully.

Behind him, Trevor groaned.

"I just left the store," Jenny answered, holding up a tea and a package of cookies as proof.

Winnie giggled. She kept staring at Dylan. It bugged him.

"Oh, yeah. Right." He didn't know what else to say.

"If you want to go in, me and Winnie will wait for you," Jenny helped.

Winnie took the sucker out of her mouth. "What?"

Jenny pushed her.

"OK. We'll be right back." Dylan almost ran in the store.

"Smooth," Trevor said.

"Shut up!"

Dylan turned down an aisle and almost ran into Gary. Gary stood with David, holding two different bags of chips. David didn't look happy to be there. He shifted from foot to foot and pushed his glasses up.

"Dylan! Hi." Gary acted as if he went to the store every day after school. "What's up?"

"Nothing."

Gary nodded. "We're just getting something before going to the park."

"What are you going to do in the park?"

Gary shrugged. He tried to act like it was no big deal, but Dylan could tell he was excited. His eyes glowed, and the corners of his mouth twitched. "Hang out. Whatever. See you."

David followed quickly after him.

Dylan almost threw his money on the counter. He pushed the door open, then halted on the sidewalk.

Josh had his arm around Gary's shoulders. "You almost got me in trouble. I didn't do anything to you. I was just kidding with you. You better learn to take a joke." Josh glanced at the crowd standing around them. He waved to Kathy and Ben. "Look, it's not my fault you can't take a joke. But don't you dare take it out on me!"

He squeezed Gary's shoulders one more time. Then, he took hold of Gary's arm and pushed him away from him. Gary stumbled and fell on the pavement.

"Got it!" Tony yelled. He kept his cell phone pointing at Gary.

Josh grinned at Dylan. "Looks like you won't have to worry about people watching your Facebook video anymore."

Gary rolled into a sitting position on the pavement, his back to the crowd. David glared at them as he helped Gary to his feet.

Tony and Josh laughed.

"It's like watching a manatee try to stand!" Josh called out.

Some people laughed. Dylan felt his insides squeeze together. His scalp prickled.

Gary took a few wobbly steps. He found his balance and walked away. Slowly at first, then faster, until he broke into a run. Faster. And faster. David followed him.

Dylan remembered Jenny. He looked around for her. She and Winnie were gone.

Dylan skated home. He spent the afternoon at Trevor's. Neither one of them felt like hanging out in the park after what happened to Gary.

Dylan wondered why Jenny left. She told him she'd wait for him.

It was dark by the time he got home. He kicked the end of his skateboard and caught it as it flew towards him. He walked across the yard and stopped when he saw a shadow by the tree.

"Gary?" he asked.

"Yeah?" Gary answered. He leaned against the tree, away from the circle of the garage light.

"Why are you standing outside?" Dylan asked.

Gary sniffed. He rubbed his nose with the back of his hand. "Not ready to go in yet."

"Oh." Dylan looked at the skateboard he held in his hands. "Uh, Gary? I'm sorry about what happened."

Gary sniffed again. "No big deal." His heel kicked the tree. "What time is it?"

"About 6:00."

Gary nodded. "They're probably sitting around the table," he said quietly, as if talking to himself.

"Huh?" Dylan asked.

"I could just walk to my room," Gary continued in a soft voice. "Tell my mom I'm not feeling well. I could just walk right past them. No one will have to know."

He shoved his hands in his pockets. He stood up and walked into the house without looking back at Dylan.

13

"Do you want another Coke?" Mr. Patterson asked.

"No, I'm good," Dylan said.

Napkins and pizza crusts littered the table. Music blared from the stereos. All around them, voices rose and fell in sync with the music's volume.

"So, school's OK, then? Your reading's coming along?"

Dylan shrugged. "I guess so."

"Well, I wouldn't worry about it," Mr. Patterson said, stretching his arms over his head. "I was never a big reader, either." He threw his napkin on his plate. "You still hanging out with Troy?"

"You mean Trevor?"

"Trevor! Yes." Mr. Patterson's face reddened. "He's OK, too?"

"Yeah, Dad, everything's fine."

Mr. Patterson took off his glasses. He cleaned them with a napkin, then put them on again.

"Jeff is having fun," he said.

Dylan looked in the same direction as his dad. Jeff ran around in circles with three other kids. It didn't even look like they were chasing each other. They just ran around in circles.

Mr. Patterson looked around. "Do you want to play some of the video games?"

Dylan shook his head. "No, thanks."

"C'mon! You don't want to just sit here, do you?" He ran his hand through his thinning hair.

Yes, Dylan thought.

He liked sitting there, just watching. That's what he did most of the time when he was with his dad. Sitting and watching TV, sitting in a movie theater, or sitting in a restaurant. His mind went blank, like it did when he skateboarded. He felt relaxed.

Mr. Patterson drummed the table with his fingertips. "Where did Kelly go with her friends tonight?"

"The football game."

"Oh, right," Mr. Patterson said, as if he should have known that. "Didn't you want to go?"

Dylan shrugged. "Not really."

"Why not?"

Dylan leaned back in his chair. "I don't know. It's boring! You don't really do anything but walk around."

Mr. Patterson nodded. "Who's Kelly hanging out with tonight?" he asked.

Dylan shrugged. "I don't know. Probably Alice and Lisa."

Mr. Patterson sighed. "One of the great things about summer is I get to see you guys more than just once a week. I'd like to see more of you than that, even. But as you're getting older, I'm seeing you less and less."

Dylan felt his insides tighten. *Was this going to be another guilt trip?* Dylan overheard Kelly once, crying to their mom after a visit with their dad because he made her feel guilty for returning a shirt he bought her.

Mr. Patterson sighed. "A part of growing up, I guess." He looked at Dylan. "Listen, if you want to spend Friday nights with your friends, I understand. It's not fair that Kelly can and you can't. Or, do you actually like hanging around Chuck E. Cheese with your little brother and your dad?"

Dylan grinned. "I guess it would be fun to go someplace else for a change."

Mr. Patterson stood up. "And I'll speak with your mother about spending time with you some Saturday afternoons instead of Friday nights. Is that OK with you?"

Dylan stood up, too. "OK, Dad. Yeah."

"Good. Go round up your brother. You can pick the movie tonight. Just nothing that's going to scare Jeff."

Will

14

Dylan waited by the lockers.

He arrived at school early, getting to his locker way before Trevor. He tried to look casual as he stared at the kids coming in. He saw Winnie move up the stairs. Jenny came in behind her.

Why does Winnie always have to be around? he thought.

He knelt down, pretending to tie his shoe. He counted to ten. Without looking around, he stood up. And banged into Winnie.

"Ow! You stepped on my foot!" She pushed him, causing him to fall into Torey.

Torey pushed him away. "Quit shoving me!"

"Sorry," Dylan mumbled. Jenny was at his locker. Taking a deep breath, he walked over to her. "Hi!"

She turned around. "Oh, hi."

Dylan swallowed. "How are you?"

"Fine."

Dylan's throat went dry. "Um, I'm sorry you had to leave yesterday."

She shut her locker. "I didn't want to see Josh beat Gary up."

"He didn't really beat him up. He just pushed him around a little, but he's all right."

"Didn't look like it to me," she said. "And I couldn't believe you didn't do anything to try to stop it."

"What could I do?" Dylan was stunned. *Why did she think he could do anything?*

"I don't know. Maybe tell Josh to stop?"

"You didn't say anything." Dylan and Jenny both turned. Trevor stood just behind Dylan. "You were there. You didn't say anything, either."

Jenny squinted her eyes. She tucked her hair behind her ears as she tried to think of something to say.

"Shut up!" was all she came up with. She stormed away from the lockers.

Trevor grabbed his things from his locker. "Forget about her. She doesn't know what the hell she's talking about."

Dylan wasn't sure.

The phone in the classroom rang. Everyone stopped talking and watched Mr. Pence answer the phone.

"Yes? Yes. Right now? OK." He turned. "Dylan? Ms. Thane wants to see you."

* * *

Ms. Thane was at her desk. "Come in, Dylan."

Dylan sat in the chair in front of her desk.

Ms. Thane pushed her glasses back into her gray hair. "Dylan, is there something happening with Gary?"

Dylan looked at her innocently. "No. What do you mean?"

"I've been getting reports he's being picked on." Ms. Thane put her glasses back on. "There was mention of something happening in the lunch room and the hallway, and then I heard about something in the park."

Dylan looked at her and shrugged. "I don't know of anything wrong."

She stared at him. He hated it when she stared at him. He felt as if she challenged him to a blinking contest.

He squirmed in his seat. "I mean, Josh teased him a little, but that was it."

Ms. Thane nodded. "I know. Both Josh and Gary told me."

So why am I here? Dylan wanted to ask. He kept quiet.

"What happened at the park yesterday?" Ms. Thane asked.

"The park?"

Ms. Thane breathed in and breathed out slowly. "Did something happen at the park between Josh and Gary?"

"No." *It happened outside the store*, he thought.

"Well, his mother called and said something happened and that Gary said you were there." She said the sentence quickly. She always did that when she couldn't nail someone for doing something.

Dylan felt bad. He didn't like how Josh treated Gary. But then he thought of Josh, Ben and Tony. Josh was always nice to Dylan. They were almost friends.

He looked at Ms. Thane. "I didn't see anything."

Ms. Thane looked at Dylan. She took a pass, and signed it. "You can go back to class."

On his way back to class, Dylan realized Gary was absent.

* * *

"Can you believe that kid?" Josh sat at his usual table in the cafeteria. He spoke loudly so everyone around him could hear. "That manatee told Ms. Thane on me. My parents have to come in and meet with her. All because someone can't take a joke! Now I'm going to get into trouble."

Dylan doubted that. Last year, Josh was accused of stealing another kid's wallet. She gave Josh three days of detention. Ms. Thane called Josh's parents that day, too. After his parents came in, he didn't have to have detention anymore.

"Gary's not even here today." Colin sat at the end of the table next to Dylan and Trevor. "How could he tell Ms. Thane if he's not even here?"

"Mind your own business, Greenhead," Tony told Colin.

"Nice comeback," Colin said. He stared at Tony.

Tony tried to stare back, but looked away a few seconds later, his face red. Josh turned his back to avoid looking at Colin.

Colin stood up. "You guys want to eat here, go right ahead. I'm not going to sit here anymore."

Dylan watched him. He was tempted to take his own tray and follow.

"Dylan, you're not going to go with that freak, are you?" Tony asked.

Dylan looked at Josh and Tony. He looked down at his tray, and kept his eyes there as he finished his pizza.

15

"You didn't miss much Friday night."

Dylan and Trevor sat in Trevor's room. Trevor scrolled through YouTube on his computer. Dylan tossed a ball in the air.

"Oh!" Trevor said. "One thing did happen, actually. Colin and Josh almost got into a fight."

Dylan forgot he tossed the ball in the air. It hit him on the head. "What happened?"

"Josh was picking on some kid. Colin told him to stop."

"Who was Colin with?"

"I don't know." Trevor frowned. "I think he went to the game by himself."

"Did anyone get in trouble?"

Trevor shook his head. "That's why I didn't think of it earlier. Nothing happened." He turned back to the computer. "Did you see Tony's video of Gary tripping on the sidewalk?"

"He didn't trip. Josh pushed him."

Trevor shrugged. "Whatever. Do you want to see it?"

"No."

Dylan remembered Gary talking to himself by the tree. For some reason, the idea of Gary's video bothered him more than the video of himself.

"Tony and Josh did a voiceover on the video. They call him a manatee on the video. It's pretty funny. You sure you don't want to see it?"

"I'm sure." He looked at Trevor. "Are we on the video?"

Trevor shook his head.

"Are you sure?"

"Just watch the damn video and see for yourself!" Trevor snapped. "What the hell's your problem? You've been acting weird all day."

Dylan sighed. "Nothing."

He didn't know what was wrong with him.

16

Kelly came home after Mr. Patterson dropped Dylan and Jeff off. She kept talking about how fun the football game was, and all the people she saw. For some reason, the conversation irritated Dylan. He spent the rest of the morning in his room, reading.

Dylan looked up from his book as Mrs. Patterson knocked, then walked into his bedroom. She sat on the edge of his bed.

Mrs. Patterson smiled. "I feel like I haven't seen you in a long time. You were with Dad on Friday, and with Trevor all day yesterday."

Dylan shrugged. "It hasn't been that long."

"Maybe not," Mrs. Patterson said, "but it feels like it." She looked around his room. He got ready for her clean-up-your-room-it's-a-mess order. "Do you ever hang out with Gary anymore?"

"Huh?" *Why did she ask that?* He shook his head.

"You two used to be friends."

"Yeah, but that was, like, 3rd grade. We haven't been friends for a long time."

"Why?"

"I don't know." Dylan put down the book he had been reading. "He's weird. He acts stupid sometimes. Like the other day, he reminded Mr. Chapin that he hadn't written down a homework assignment. And... I don't know. He just looks and acts goofy."

Mrs. Patterson nodded as she stared at her hands. "His mother called me yesterday."

"She did?"

"Uh-huh. She said he came home Thursday night with scrapes on his face and arm. She didn't know until Friday morning, when he said he was too sick to go to school."

"Oh," Dylan said. His face felt hot, and he felt prickly around his scalp. "Did he say what happened?"

"That's why she called. She wanted to know if you knew what happened." Mrs. Patterson looked Dylan straight in the eye. "Do you?"

"No. Why would I know?"

Mrs. Patterson continued to look at him. She looked at him the way Ms. Thane looked at him. "You're sure you don't know?"

"Yes, I'm sure!" Dylan tried not to sound defensive. He always sounded defensive whenever he lied.

Mrs. Patterson leaned back slightly. "Gary's mom also said that he likes you. She said he talks about you."

Damn, he thought. *Why did she have to tell him that?*

He shrugged. "It's not like I hate him. I just don't like him."

Mrs. Patterson stood up. At the door, she turned and faced him. "You've heard the expression 'we have a will of our own,' right?"

Dylan nodded.

"That doesn't really matter," she continued, "if we don't act like we do. Tomorrow, I want you to clean your room."

She shut his door.

Dylan decided to call Trevor.

Trevor's mom said Dylan was allowed to spend the night, so he did. Dylan liked Trevor's parents, but he always felt weird being at their house. He thought it was weird whenever he went to someone's house where there were two parents. He was used to living with just his mom.

That said, Trevor had a TV and a computer in his room.

It was on the computer, long after dinner, that they saw the Facebook post from Josh.

Hey, manatee. Your day is coming. Monday you'll be washed up for sure. Do everyone a favor and beach yourself. Save us all the hassle. Even Greenpeace won't bother to save your sorry ass.

After Josh posted his threat on Facebook, they watched as others joined the conversation. Most people told Josh he was funny and that they loved how he called Gary a manatee. Tony said he would help Josh take down Gary.

They stared at the computer. Another comment was posted.

"Hey! That's Jenny!" Dylan leaned in closer.

Shows you guys are really tough. Threatening people on the internet. Why don't you get a life?! she wrote.

A moment later, another comment: *Shut the hell up.*

Then: *Mind your own business, skank.*

"Whoa. This is getting weird," Trevor said. He moved back, away from the computer. "What do you think we should do?"

Trevor closed the website. They sat quietly, staring at the screen.

"Do you think we should do something?"

"Like what?"

Trevor shrugged. "Let's go on Netflix."

Dylan regretted not telling his mom. *But what would she do? Call the school in the morning? Call Josh's parents?* Josh didn't get in trouble after his parents came to school Friday.

His eyes roamed over the piles of clothes on the floor, the books and paper on the desk, and the poster of Jackie Robinson on the wall above Trevor's desk.

Maybe he should tell his mom.

Even though the clock read only 8:20, he turned off the light and climbed under the covers.

Suddenly, he was tired.

17

Dylan dropped his skateboard on the pavement. A clump of kids stood outside the store. A few others tossed a football at the far end of the parking lot.

He kicked off with his foot. He headed toward the park. There, another clump of students gathered in a circle. He slowed down.

Trevor and John stood at the back, standing on their toes to try to see.

"What's going on?" Dylan asked.

"Fight," Trevor said, stretching his neck to see better. "Tony and Gary."

"Actually, it's more like Tony beating the shit out of Gary," John corrected.

There was no way Dylan could see over everyone's heads. He moved around the circle until he found a small opening. He wiggled his way through.

"Get up, Gary!" Tony's eyes squinted. He clenched his fists so tight the veins in his arms looked like they were going to explode.

Gary lay on the ground, curled up in a ball. His eyes were closed. Dylan saw his lips moving, but no sound came out. Dylan looked at the other kids circled around Tony and Gary.

No one spoke. They all had the same expression: noses crinkled, eyebrows furrowed. He looked over the crowd a second time. He stopped and stared. He thought he saw Josh hiding behind a tree a few yards away.

"I said get up!" Tony kicked Gary in the leg.

Gary squealed, but kept his eyes closed.

"So, you're gonna lie there?" Tony demanded. He grabbed Gary's shirt.

"Stop it!"

"Who said that?" Tony dropped Gary's shirt. He turned to Dylan, stunned. "You?"

Dylan nodded. "Leave him alone. He didn't do anything to you."

"He keeps getting Josh and me in trouble." Tony looked at Gary in disgust. "He's a pathetic rodent."

I thought he was a manatee, Dylan thought. "If you and Josh left him alone, you wouldn't get into trouble."

Tony picked up his sweatshirt from the ground. He wiped his hands on his red t-shirt. The other kids slowly peeled away from the scene.

"You—" Tony began, then stopped.

Colin stood next to Trevor and John.

Tony smirked, then walked toward the spot where Dylan thought he saw Josh.

Colin helped Gary to his feet. "Are you OK, Gary?"

Gary nodded. He rolled up his pants leg. His leg was bruised from where Tony kicked him. He also bruised his shoulder when Tony pushed him to the ground. Other than that, he seemed OK. Gary looked at Dylan, then down at the ground.

"Thanks," he mumbled.

Dylan was also embarrassed. "Don't mention it," he said.

No one seemed to know what to do, or how to leave.

"Gary!" David ran into the park from the parking lot. "I...." He leaned forward, placing his hands on his knees. "I didn't see you waiting for the bus.... Overheard someone say something about the park." He coughed.

Trevor and John pounded him on the back.

"I'm OK," Gary said. He picked up his backpack. "Do you think your parents can pick us up?"

David nodded, still wheezing. They walked out of the park, back toward the school.

On the way home, Trevor told Dylan the story. Tony somehow convinced Gary to go outside with him. To say sorry or something. Once they were in the park, he started yelling at him.

"When did you get there?"

"Me and John followed them. It was weird, seeing Tony and Gary walking together, you know?"

"I saw Josh hiding behind some trees," Dylan said.

"Yeah, I saw him, too."

* * *

During dinner, Kelly talked on and on about her day. Jeff talked about his favorite TV show. They both talked so much that no one noticed how quiet Dylan was.

After dinner, Jeff and Kelly fought over who was going to use the computer. Dylan went back to his room. He finished his homework, then went to bed.

18

Dylan slumped at the table. "I don't want to go to school, Mom."

Without turning around from the stove, Mrs. Patterson said, "You're going."

"C'mon, Mom!" Dylan whined. "I never stay home from school. Why can't I just stay home this one time?"

"I want to stay home, too!" Jeff yelled.

Mrs. Patterson placed a plate of toast on the table. "Nobody is staying home today. Now hurry up and eat. I have to be at work early today."

Kelly piled her books on the table. She reached for a glass, moving close to Dylan. "Who's 'manatee?'" she whispered. She wasn't laughing, or even smiling. "It's Gary, isn't it?" she said, even lower.

"How did you..."

Kelly placed her finger over her lips and looked at their mother.

Mrs. Patterson poured herself a cup of coffee. "Hurry and get dressed, Jeff. Molly's mom said she'd take you to school. I have to drop you off in about 15 minutes."

She took her coffee and left the room.

"How did you know?" Dylan asked.

Kelly pulled her hair in a ponytail. "Stacey was at the deli on Thursday. And Amy got the pictures of Josh pushing Gary on her phone."

"Oh."

"What's going to happen today?"

Dylan shrugged. "I have no idea."

Kelly grabbed a piece of toast. "Just don't get involved. Josh is a jerk."

Dylan looked up. "I thought you liked Josh! You said last year he was cute."

"I meant that in a little kid kind of way," Kelly explained, "at the beginning of the year. I like his sister, Beth. Josh is obnoxious."

For some reason, that made Dylan feel better.

"You should hang around with Colin," Kelly said.

"Huh? I thought you said he was weird."

Kelly shrugged. "Well, he is. Sort of. But he's cool." She grabbed her books. "Bye, Mom!" she yelled.

* * *

"Jenny deleted her comment."

Dylan stood behind Trevor, waiting for him to finish with his locker. "When? Last night?"

"I guess so. You didn't go on it last night?"

Dylan shook his head. He didn't tell Trevor he thought about closing his Facebook account entirely.

Trevor slammed his locker shut. "You want me to wait for you?"

"Go ahead. I'll see you at lunch."

19

Dylan slowly put his books away. On the other side of the art room, Gary pulled out his notebooks and dropped them on the floor.

"Hey, Gary!"

"Hi." Gary didn't look at him.

"How are you feeling?"

"OK," he mumbled.

Dylan shifted his books from his right to his left arm. "Um..."

"I'm sorry my mom called your mom," Gary interrupted him. "I didn't ask her to do that."

"I know," Dylan assured him.

Gary shut his locker and faced him. "I just want you to know I had nothing to do with that," he said.

Dylan was surprised. Gary looked so old. Behind his glasses, his eyes had no light. His face was pale. The corners of his mouth drooped down. A patch of jagged red lines covered his left cheek. Last week, his face had looked round and babyish. Today, it looked long and thin.

"See ya." Gary turned and walked down the hall, away from Dylan.

Dylan spent the morning in a fog. He couldn't get Gary's image out of his mind. He felt removed from everyone else.

Conversations around him involved what people did over the weekend and what TV shows were watched. He heard whispers of Gary's name and Josh's name.

When he saw Jenny, it was like he was looking at her from a distance. Her gray hoodie blended with the background. He made sure he sat away from Josh.

It worked, until lunch time.

"Care if we sit here?" Josh, Sarah, and Tony plopped their trays next to Trevor and Dylan.

"How come you didn't go to the game?" Tony asked Dylan.

"I was—" Dylan started.

"Hey, does anyone know that Jenny... what's-her-name? The new girl?"

"Yeah, I know her," Sarah said. She rolled her eyes. "Please!"

Ben and Laura squeezed between Tony and Dylan, forcing Dylan to the very edge of the bench.

"What's wrong with her?"

"Who?"

"The new girl, Jenny."

Laura snickered. "You know why she hangs out with Winnie? Because nobody else will hang out with her. She acts like she's all Miss Perfect."

Sarah shrugged her shoulders. "She's just your basic nobody."

"You know her, right, Dylan?" Josh asked. "I mean, I've seen you talking to her before."

"Save yourself, Dylan!" Laura begged. The others laughed.

Colin stared at Dylan. For a moment, the two locked eyes. Colin rose, threw his trash out, and walked out of the cafeteria.

* * *

The bell rang. Students streamed out of the rooms and into the hallways. Backpacks, jackets, and books swirled behind lockers. For five minutes, the noise level grew louder and louder. Then, suddenly, everything quieted. As if by magic, the hallways were empty, with only a few stragglers cramming what they could into their backpacks.

Dylan was the last one out of the social studies room. He waited against the wall for the hallways to clear before going to his locker. Trevor was already gone. Dylan wanted to get his things and just go home.

The day was cloudy. On sunny days, the school looked dark. On cloudy days, the fluorescent lights shone brighter than usual.

The lockers glowed as Dylan passed them on the way out of the building. He saw Ms. Thane in her office. He stopped. He thought of going in. Just to say hi. He wasn't sure why he wanted to. It just felt right.

He took a step towards her room. Her phone rang.

Dylan continued his way out of the building.

20

"ARRGGHH!"

Dylan's arm shot out from under his covers toward Jeff.

"Mom! Dylan's trying to hit me!" Jeff ran into the kitchen.

Dylan yanked his jeans off the floor where he'd thrown them when he got undressed last night for bed.

He pulled on a sweatshirt. Looking in the mirror, he put on his baseball cap.

"Do you still not want to go to school?" Mrs. Patterson asked.

Dylan shrugged. It wasn't bad yesterday. From the kitchen window, he watched the school bus pull away from the curb.

He rode his skateboard through the park. The buses lined up outside the school, dumping their load of students. Dylan pushed his way through the crowded hallways. He saw Josh and Tony laughing with Laura and Kim. Josh waved at him.

"Trevor!" Dylan called, nearing his locker. "Hurry up and get your stuff. I'm going to be late!"

"I'm trying! Oops. Sorry, Mattie."

Today was Tuesday. Mr. Pence was first period. Jenny sat two rows away from him in Mr. Pence's class.

"Hi, Dylan," Gary said. He sat in the front row of Mr. Pence's class.

"Hi."

Josh and Tony followed Dylan into the classroom. They ignored Gary.

Dylan sat down at his desk and pulled out his notebook.

"Hi, Dylan." Jenny stood next to him. "I heard about what happened yesterday," she said in a low voice. "That was really cool, what you did."

Dylan blushed. "Thanks." He swallowed. "I thought it was pretty cool what you wrote on Facebook. Why did you delete it?"

"My mom came in the room when I was on. She saw what was happening and made me delete it."

"Oh." *Say something, you idiot!* he thought.

"Maybe we can meet up after school," she suggested.

She unzipped her hoodie. She was wearing her pink sweater.

Dylan shrugged. "OK," he said, smiling. "Sure."

About The Author

Cynthia Kerns is an instructional designer at Messiah University in Pennsylvania, where she uses infomation technology to enhance the learning process. She's a long-time member of Educause, a nonprofit association and the largest community of technology, academic, industry, and campus leaders advancing higher education through the use of IT.Besides writing and teaching about rocks, Brian enjoys playing guitar and banjo, reading (just about anything), road trips, astronomy, and pizza.

About The Publisher

Story Shares is a nonprofit focused on supporting the millions of teens and adults who struggle with reading by creating a new shelf in the library specifically for them. The ever-growing collection features content that is compelling and culturally relevant for teens and adults, yet still readable at a range of lower reading levels.

Story Shares generates content by engaging deeply with writers, bringing together a community to create this new kind of book. With more intriguing and approachable stories to choose from, the teens and adults who have fallen behind are improving their skills and beginning to discover the joy of reading. For more information, visit storyshares.org.

Easy to Read. Hard to Put Down.

www.ingramcontent.com/pod-product-compliance
Lightning Source LLC
Chambersburg PA
CBHW051303170626
46809CB00004B/1760

* 9 7 8 1 6 4 2 6 1 2 2 2 6 *